STARS OF THE NEGRO LEAGUES

Josh Gibson

Catcher and Power Hitter

STARS OF THE NEGRO LEAGUES

Josh Gibson

Catcher and Power Hitter

Hallie Murray

Enslow Publishing
101 W. 23rd Street
Suite 240
New York, NY 10011
USA
enslow.com

Published in 2020 by Enslow Publishing, LLC.
101 W. 23rd Street, Suite 240, New York, NY 10011

Cataloging-in-Publication Data

Names: Murray, Hallie.

Title: Josh Gibson: catcher and power hitter / Hallie Murray

Description: New York : Enslow Publishing, 2020. | Series: Stars of the negro leagues | Includes bibliographic references and index. | Audience: Grades 7–12.

Identifiers: ISBN 9781978510531 (library bound) | ISBN 9781978510524 (pbk.)

Subjects: LCSH: Gibson, Josh, 1911–1947—Juvenile literature. | Baseball players—United States—Biography—Juvenile literature. | African American baseball players—United States—Biography—Juvenile literature. | Negro leagues—History—Juvenile literature.

Classification: LCC GV865.G53 M87 2020 | DDC 796.357092 [B]—dc23

Printed in the United States of America

To Our Readers: We have done our best to make sure all website addresses in this book were active and appropriate when we went to press. However, the author and the publisher have no control over and assume no liability for the material available on those websites or on any websites they may link to. Any comments or suggestions can be sent by email to customerservice@enslow.com.

Portions of this book originally appeared in *Josh Gibson* by Nick Twemlow.

Photo Credits: Cover, p. 3 (inset photo Josh Gibson), pp. 13, 22–23, 33, 46–47, 62, 72–73, 76 Transcendental Graphics/Getty Images; cover, pp. 3, 7, 12, 28, 44, 60, 75 (background) Library of Congress Prints and Photographs Division; cover, p. 3 (bat and ball) Mike Flippo/Shutterstock.com; pp. 8, 24–25, 37, 50–51, 53, 58, 68–69, 80–81, 85 National Baseball Hall of Fame and Museum; pp. 10, 88–89 © AP Images; pp. 14–15 Stock Montage/Archive Photos/Getty Images; pp. 16–17 Universal History Archive/UIG/Bridgeman Images; p. 19 Walter Oleksy/Alamy Stock Photo; pp. 30–31 Everett Collection Historical/Alamy Stock Photo; pp. 40–41 Clarence Gatson/Gado/Archive Photos/Getty Images; pp. 54–55 Bettmann/Getty Images; pp. 64–65 Teenie Harris Archive/Carnegie Museum of Art/Getty Images; cover, pp. 1, 3 (baseball graphic) Kano07/Shutterstock.com; interior pages (glove) Sergiy1975/Shutterstock.com; interior pages (diamond graphic) Viktorija Reuta/Shutterstock.com.

Contents

Introduction

Most people have heard of the great Babe Ruth, but far fewer people have heard of Josh Gibson, the Negro Leagues player whose hitting ability matched—and maybe even surpassed—that of the Bambino himself. During his brilliant career, Josh Gibson barely registered a blip on the American baseball radar screen. The man often called the "Black Babe Ruth" slipped through his short life barely noticed by a baseball-crazy American public. Admired by his fellow players, and perhaps the most powerful home-run hitter ever to put a bat to a ball, Gibson hit an estimated 900 homers over his career.

In contrast to his occasional teammate and frequent rival, Satchel Paige, Gibson remained a quiet and mysterious figure to both fans and historians. Paige was a colorful figure with a larger-than-life personality, and when he squared up against the stoic, powerful Gibson, fans were in for a treat. But after his untimely death at the age of thirty-five, Gibson largely faded away.

Josh Gibson was one of the most famous Negro Leagues players of his day. Here he is in the 1930s in a catching stance in his Pittsburgh Crawfords uniform.

Gibson officially died from a stroke after years of headaches and dizziness caused by a brain tumor, but according to baseball legend, Gibson died of a broken heart. Gibson was considered one of the best players in the Negro Leagues, if not the very best, but when it came to breaking the Major League Baseball color line, he was overlooked in favor of a young player named Jackie Robinson. It's said that the heartbreak of missing the chance to play in the majors is what killed Gibson in the end, though his struggles with alcohol and drugs were probably the real culprit.

Gibson started playing baseball as a kid when his family moved to Pittsburgh, Pennsylvania. He idolized players on the local team, the Homestead Grays, and after dropping out of school after finishing ninth grade, Gibson started playing with recreational teams in the Pittsburgh area. He was a big deal on these teams, both in terms of physical size and in talent, and soon gained a reputation as a good catcher and, maybe more importantly, a powerful hitter whose homeruns went farther than anyone else's in his league.

Thanks to a series of improbable circumstances, Gibson ended up playing for the Grays starting in July 1930. He spent most of his career with the Grays and gained a reputation as a phenomenal power hitter and great catcher. But Gibson's personal life was marked by tragedy. His first wife died during childbirth the same year he joined the Grays, and he was never really able to be there for his children. Later in life, he struggled with alcohol dependency and likely abused drugs like heroin and other narcotics, which didn't help his health. Gibson was diagnosed with a brain tumor in 1943 but didn't want to have surgery, so he spent

Gibson passed away on January 20, 1947, less than a month after his thirty-fifth birthday. He is buried in Allegheny Cemetery in Pittsburgh, Pennsylvania.

the next four years with bad headaches and other difficulties. In January 1947, he passed away, just after turning thirty-five.

In 1971, Gibson was posthumously inducted into the Baseball Hall of Fame, the second player to be inducted based on his career in the Negro Leagues. The first primarily Negro Leagues player to be inducted was none other than Gibson's longtime rival, Satchel Paige. Gibson's son, Josh Jr., also played for the Homestead Grays and helped honor his father's legacy through the Josh Gibson Foundation, which supports youth athletics and academics. Though Gibson was overlooked for a long time, in recent years, he's been better recognized in history and in art. There's even been an opera written about him! Called *The Summer King*, it premiered in April 2017 in Pittsburgh.

By looking back at Gibson's life and the lives of other significant Negro Leagues players, we can gain a better understanding of the history of baseball and the effects of segregation in the sport and in the wider culture. Maybe one day the names of Negro Leagues greats like Josh Gibson, Buck Leonard, Satchel Paige, Cool Papa Bell, and many others will be as famous to baseball fans as those of white legends like Babe Ruth. The only way to make sure that happens is to keep telling their stories and remembering the history, both good and bad, that got us to where we are today.

Chapter 1

The Early Days of Baseball

The first recorded baseball game took place in Hoboken, New Jersey, on June 19, 1846, between the Knickerbocker Base Ball Club of New York and the New York Base Ball Club. Baseball, then a brand new sport resembling the British game of cricket, looked pretty different from the way it is today. The rules would barely be recognizable by today's standards. While today pitchers throw overhand from sixty feet and six inches away, back then pitchers threw underhand from a distance of forty-five feet, dangerously close to the hitter. Pitchers tried to get the batters, or "strikers" as they were called, out on four strikes. Fly balls caught were an out, but a foul ball caught on one bounce was also an out. Players played barehanded, and games would be over if one team scored twenty-one runs, rather than today's nine-inning structure.

At that point, baseball wasn't so much a sport as it was an upper-class leisure activity. Teams were usually made up of wealthy white men,

Alexander Cartwright Jr. helped found the New York Knickerbockers Base Ball Club and is sometimes referred to as the "father of baseball."

and games were often an excuse for picnics and dances. Because they were grand social events, both men and women attended the games in great number, and over the next decade baseball's popularity soared.

The Growth of a Game

In 1858, the National Association of Base Ball Players (NABBL) was founded in order to protect the interests of amateur baseball in New York City. By the 1860s, it had grown into a national organization. Its members would pay dues, and the NABBL would set rules and admit teams into the association. Although the association's rules were haphazardly adopted, the NABBL provided baseball with a national public image and helped make the sport even more popular. This was great for white baseball teams, but teams with black players didn't benefit because

This engraving of spectators watching a baseball game, entitled "The New Grounds of the Metropolitan Baseball Club on Staten Island," shows fans in their nicest clothes socializing during the game.

African American teams started forming in the late nineteenth century, after white teams began to exclude black players from their rosters. This photo of a Danbury, Connecticut, team was taken in 1880.

they weren't even allowed to join the association. Just like American society at large, baseball at that time was segregated.

This didn't stop black men from playing baseball, of course. Baseball historian Harry Simmons notes that the first official all-African American baseball game took place in 1860 in Brooklyn, New York, fourteen years after the first recorded all-white baseball game took place at Elysian Fields

in Hoboken. Two African American teams, Weeksville of New York and the Colored Union Club, played a full nine-inning game, with Weeksville winning 11- 0.

By 1865, a loose organization of African American baseball teams had also sprung up across the East and throughout the Middle-Atlantic states. Unlike the white baseball teams, which were mostly made up of wealthy young men with time on their hands, these teams, including the Monitor Club of Jamaica (New York), the Bachelors of Albany (New York), the Excelsiors of Philadelphia, and the Unique Club of Chicago, were composed mainly of soldiers who had fought in the Civil War.

By the late 1860s, the Pythians, a team formed by two ex-cricket players and promoted by former army major Octavius V. Catto, formed in Philadelphia. The team quickly became known as a powerhouse, soundly beating most of the other African American baseball teams. Finding a ball field for African American games in Philadelphia could be difficult, so the Pythians often invited teams to play their games out of town.

Octavius Catto decided to broach the question of integration in 1867. He dispatched Raymond C. Burr as his representative to the NABBL's annual convention in Philadelphia to ask for official recognition of the Pythians team. Though the white Philadelphia Athletics seconded Catto's petition, NABBL refused. The association issued the following statement: "It is not presumed by your Committee that any club who have applied are composed of persons of color, or any portion of them; and the recommendations of your Committee in this report are based upon this view, and they unanimously report against the admission of any club which may be composed of one or more colored persons." The association made this move, it claimed, not as a sign of racial prejudice but to avoid "subjects having a political bearing."

The Rise of the Professional Leagues

African American baseball experienced moderate successes over the next couple of years, including several white-versus-African American games that were wildly popular and financially successful. Unfortunately, the death of Octavius Catto, who had become a powerful African American rights activist in Philadelphia, signaled the end of organized

Octavius Catto was a civil rights activist in Philadelphia who campaigned for emancipation and equal rights for African Americans. He was murdered during a fight on Election Day in 1871.

African American baseball. Catto, who was murdered at the age of thirty-two by a white man, had been African American baseball's biggest promoter. Even the Pythians folded, and African American baseball quietly faded away.

Oddly enough, over the next twenty years, white baseball offered the only (albeit limited) opportunities for African American players. The creation of a professional organization, the National Association of Professional Base Ball Players (NAPBBL), weakened the power of the NABBL. The NAPBBL was intent on changing the amateur atmosphere of baseball. They hoped to turn it into a profitable, organized business.

African American teams were nonexistent in the association, but a few African American players managed to find their way onto teams. In 1884, Moses Fleetwood "Fleet" Walker, a college-educated ballplayer, became the first African American to play in the majors. John "Bud" Fowler became baseball's first widely known African American player when, at the age of fourteen, he played second base for a white team in New Castle, Pennsylvania.

Fowler, a highly accomplished player, carried the extra burden of having to constantly prove himself to his white counterparts, a recurring theme for African American players for years to come. An African American player of this era faced racism in the form of white major league players, managers, owners, and fans. A silent "gentleman's agreement" between major league clubs made the prospect of an African American player playing professional baseball exceptionally unlikely. Many white executives simply agreed to this policy without putting it in writing. Some team owners, motivated more often by their desire to win than any sense of justice, kept African American players on their teams, though they put themselves at great risk by doing so.

But the few African American men playing in the minor and major leagues, such as Fowler and Walker, could not be ignored. Quite simply, they played some of the best ball anybody had ever seen in the game's then brief history. Fowler's considerable skills forced even white newspaper reporters to notice him. In 1885, *Sporting Life* magazine called him "one of the best general players in the country... If he had a white face, he would be playing with the best of them."

Some African American business leaders, impressed by the glowing praise players such as Fowler and Walker received in several white newspapers, attempted to put together leagues of African American teams. Among the limited successes in these attempts was the Southern League, composed of ten teams from across the South. The league was formed in 1886 and played out one full season before folding the next year. Financially unable to continue, the league did revive interest in all-African American professional teams. Over the next few years, the biggest presence of African American ballplayers came in the form of an independent team, the Cuban Giants.

The First African American Teams

Formed in 1885, the Giants were a team of African American players who had formerly worked as waiters and porters at the Argyle Hotel in Long Island, New York—not in Cuba. By calling the team "Cuban," the team's white financial backers hoped to improve the team's chances of appealing to

SYRACUSE
SYRACUSE

The Syracuse Stars Base Ball Club was an integrated minor league baseball team in the late 1800s. Moses Fleetwood Walker, who played in the major leagues with the Toledo Blue Stockings in 1884, is in the back row on the far right.

white audiences. While most white baseball fans dismissed the thought of watching an African American team play, promoters hoped that some of them might come to see black baseball players from Cuba. As these players were supposedly foreign-born, white fans could feel safe in supporting them despite the societal rules of segregation. The players tried to act like they were from Cuba, even going so far as speaking in "Spanish sounding" words on the playing field.

Initially created to entertain white vacationers, the team, under the guidance of white promoter John F. Lang, turned professional and went on to play as barnstormers. Barnstormers were teams who traveled across the country, from small towns to big cities, playing against any willing opponent. These teams often played many games in one day, and just as often played against the biggest and best white teams of the time. In the absence of a proven league, barnstorming became the only way for African American baseball teams to play regularly and earn money.

At the same time, players like Fowler and Walker were playing in the International League, composed mostly of teams from New York. African American players were often subject to hostility from fans, opposing teams, and even

The Cuban Giants, formed in 1885 and pictured in this 1895 photo, were one of the first all-black baseball teams in the United States. Despite the name, none of the players were actually from Cuba.

Plessy v. Ferguson

America was largely segregated after the Civil War, but segregation was not enforced on a federal level until a ruling called *Plessy v. Ferguson*. In 1892, a man named Homer Plessy bought a first-class train ticket and boarded a "whites only" train car in Louisiana. Because he was one-eighth African American, he was asked to get off and move to the "colored" car. Plessy refused to move and was arrested. In his case, lawyers argued that removing Plessy from the railroad car was a violation of his Thirteenth and Fourteenth Amendment rights. The case, known as *Plessy v. Ferguson*, went to the highest court in America, the Supreme Court, in 1896. Unfortunately, Plessy lost, and the Court ruled that public organizations could have separate facilities for black and white people as long as the facilities were "equal." Of course, the facilities were never equal, and the idea of "separate, but equal" spaces created inequality and really limited black people's civil rights. Since then, cases like *Brown v. Board of Education* (1954) have made segregation illegal.

their own teammates. Many whites-only teams would withdraw from a game against a team that fielded even one African American player.

If they did play, many players on whites-only teams attempted to injure African American players. The practice of a base runner sliding forcefully into second base and aiming his spiked shoes at the second baseman developed during this time. White players hoped to injure African American player Horace Phillips. Phillips would later strap wooden splints around his shins for protection.

The early history of African American baseball is part mystery, part myth, and wholly bound up in the question of race in America. The end of the Civil War did not mean the end of racism and inequality in America, nor did the signing of the Compromise of 1887 by the US Congress and President Grover Cleveland. Instead, these acts officially ended Reconstruction and removed all legal obstacles to Jim Crow in the South. The effect was to reinforce racial segregation, particularly in the South. As the leading newspaper of the North, the *New York Times*, wrote, "Northern men no longer denounce the suppression of the Negro vote [in the South] as it used to be denounced in the Reconstruction days. The necessity of it under the supreme law of self-preservation is candidly recognized." Finally, the 1896 Supreme Court decision in *Plessy v. Ferguson* supported "separate but equal" public accommodations. Due to prejudice and discrimination, though, such accommodations were separate but wholly unequal.

Chapter 2

In the Sandlots of Pittsburgh

Josh Gibson was born on December 21, 1911, in a small town in Georgia called Buena Vista. Georgia was not the friendliest state for African Americans. Gibson's father was sharecropper, and the South held few opportunities for black Americans. When Gibson was eleven years old, his family moved to Pittsburgh, Pennsylvania, which is where Gibson first started playing organized baseball.

Though slavery had ended, the late nineteenth and early twentieth centuries were still difficult for African Americans. The end of the Civil War and the Reconstruction era that followed helped to free enslaved African Americans and restore some of their rights, but the the roots of racism ran deep throughout all of America, especially in the South. Soon after the Civil War, new laws, known as Jim Crow, were enacted that continued to limit the rights and opportunities of black Americans. By 1900, life for African Americans in the South was one of low wages, sixty- or seventy-hour workweeks, and little more than hope.

From the 1880s well into the 1960s, American states enforced segregation through such laws. Across the country, these laws marginalized African Americans. For example, African Americans could not lawfully dine in the same room in a restaurant as whites, nor could they use the same restroom facilities. Interracial marriages were declared illegal. If an African American family wanted to attend the circus in Louisiana, they would purchase their tickets at a different booth than white people, and would watch the show in an entirely different tent.

Though the effect of Jim Crow was felt most deeply in the South, northern states often passed Jim Crow laws, too. In fact, the state of Massachusetts enacted the first such law in 1841, forbidding African Americans and whites to travel in the same railroad car. But many African Americans still considered the North a better place to live because the growing industrial centers found in such places as Pittsburgh, Pennsylvania, and New York City offered many opportunities for work.

Moving North

It was this promise of work that led Josh's father, Mark Gibson, to uproot his family from their home in Buena Vista and take them to Pittsburgh. A sharecropper, Mark Gibson had heard the stories of prosperous African American communities forming in these cities. In 1921, he set out alone for Pittsburgh, then known as the Smoky City, and tried to gain employment in the massive steel industry there.

Shortly after arriving, he found a job with the giant Carnegie-Illinois Steel plant. Two years later, he sent for his wife, Nancy, and three children, Josh, (born December

Pittsburgh in 1920 was home to a booming steel industry that provided people of all races with steady jobs and large communities.

11, 1911); Jerry, (born in 1914); and a daughter, Annie, (born in 1917). The family moved into the Pleasant Valley neighborhood on the city's North Side. Their split from the South was complete.

For Josh Gibson, Pittsburgh offered a vast playground of streets and sandlots, and he soon established himself as one of the neighborhood's best athletes. He was stocky and thick, but a fast runner and powerful swimmer. And though he had played baseball only a few times in Georgia, there were numerous opportunities for him to pick up a bat and swing at baseball games in Pleasant Valley.

The lure of baseball and his growing skill at the game would soon lead Josh out of school. As he said much later in his life, "The greatest gift Dad gave me was to get me out of the South." And since Josh was nearing his full size of six feet one inch and 215 pounds, he was already a presence on the field.

Having completed the fifth grade in Georgia, Josh continued school in Pittsburgh in the Allegheny Pre-Vocational School, where teachers steered him toward electrical studies. But as the professional prospects for African American baseball players increased, along with the possibility that a young African American boy could become a professional ballplayer, the lure of the game became irresistible. For Josh and other young boys in

Pleasant Valley, the team that filled their dreams was known as the Homestead Grays.

Cum Posey and the Homestead Grays

Located just east of Pittsburgh, Homestead, Pennsylvania, is a steel mill town. In the early part of the twentieth century, many steelworkers were also great ballplayers. The best of them played for the Murdock Grays—an integrated team that challenged, and usually beat, other local teams. But the team was transformed that year when a young man fresh out of Penn State University named Cumberland Willis Posey ("Cum" to his teammates) joined them. Within two years of joining, he was made captain. Posey also worked at organizing the Grays, by then called the Homestead Grays, into a semiprofessional team.

Posey was a creative and fierce manager and promoter. He successfully fought to repeal the ban on playing Sunday ballgames. In this way, he increased the number of games the team could play, thereby increasing the amount of money they could earn. This rise in revenue enabled Posey to put his players on salary by 1922. When Posey signed the well-known African American pitcher Smokey Joe Williams, who brought with him a storied history from his play with African American teams in Chicago and New York, the Grays were headed for the big time. They became the most popular African American team in Pennsylvania.

Under Posey's firm guidance, by the late 1920s the Grays became a profitable organization. The historical importance of their success, on and off the field, cannot be underestimated. African American fans packed games to

Smokey Joe Williams was known as one of the greatest pitchers in the Negro Leagues. He spent twenty-five years playing baseball professionally, from 1907 to 1932.

cheer the Grays' no-nonsense brand of baseball, and their winning ways made them heroes to the kids of Homestead and Pittsburgh, including Josh Gibson.

Creating a National League

Interestingly, Posey and the Grays were not a part of organized African American baseball, which was headed at that time by Rube Foster, a Chicagoan who had once been a talented pitcher. Foster turned to organizing and owning teams in Chicago in the early part of the 1900s. Foster aimed to create a Negro league, composed of established African American teams from northern cities, that would equal the white baseball leagues.

The Negro National League (NNL) consisted of Foster's own Chicago American Giants, the Cuban Stars, the Dayton Marcos, the Chicago Giants, the Indianapolis ABCs, the Kansas City Monarchs, the Detroit Stars, and the St. Louis Giants.

The NNL experienced the usual growing pains a new business suffers, but it persisted and succeeded as no other African American baseball league had before. A rival organization, the Eastern Colored League (ECL), formed in 1923. Instead of joining forces with Foster's NNL, the ECL fought bitterly for the same players, franchises (teams), and fans. Over the next decade, this competition nearly destroyed both leagues.

What was Cum Posey doing with his Homestead Grays during all of this? He was sitting back, observing this competition and the destructive effects it was having not only on the leagues' survival but on all of African American baseball. He was keenly aware that if the Grays joined

Code Names

Including the Chicago American Giants, there were more than two dozen African American baseball teams called the Giants, both before this time and after. Many newspapers refused to run pictures of African American people, so when readers saw the word "Giants," they recognized it as a code word for a game involving an African American team. Other teams, like the Atlanta Black Crackers (later the Indianapolis ABCs), the Washington Black Senators, and the New York Black Yankees, included race right in their names. The Negro Leagues were hugely important to the social lives of many African Americans, so it was important that team names were easily recognizable to fans and potential fans. Going to a baseball game was a big social event and brought communities together, and watching African Americans succeed in professional baseball proved empowering in other aspects of African Americans' lives as well.

one or the other league, his own control of the team would weaken. In fact, Foster was losing control of his own league, as he suffered from mental illness. By 1926, he was unable to function from day to day. He was hospitalized and died at the age of fifty-one in 1930.

Foster had given African American baseball a forceful and necessary push. Though the NNL folded in 1932, as did the Eastern Colored League four years earlier, a new league emerged: the American Negro League. Cum Posey finally decided that his Grays would join. This marked the beginning of Posey's impressive political influence on all Negro League baseball.

From the Sandlots to the Sox

Josh Gibson left Allegheny Pre-Vocational School at the age of sixteen, having completed the ninth grade. He took up various jobs, apprenticing in an air brakes manufacturing plant, moving on to a steel mill, even working in a department store. Leaving school was probably not a difficult decision for Gibson, though he was a mild-mannered and likeable teenager by all accounts. But his family didn't place an emphasis on education, and a family such as his, intimately familiar with the poverty of the South, was more interested in making ends meet. Indeed, the Gibsons learned that African American poverty was not just a Southern problem, but an American one.

By 1927, Gibson had established his reputation as a ballplayer in the sandlots scattered about Pleasant Valley. In fact, Gibson's entry into organized baseball came that year, when he joined a North Side team called the Pleasant Valley Red Sox; shortly thereafter, he joined an all-African

Josh Gibson is best known for his powerful hitting, but he was also a great catcher. His catching gear included a mask, chest padding, and shin guards.

American recreational team. He played catcher, the position he would play for the rest of his baseball career. Because of his considerable size and strength, as well as his quickness and keen reflexes, Gibson was well suited for the position. The following year, Gibson helped organize the Crawford Colored Giants along with Harry Beale, another North Side player. Gibson also played for the team.

The Pittsburgh Crawfords

The Crawfords, a team based in Pittsburgh, played a tougher, more skilled game of baseball than most sandlot teams. Though they went pro in 1931, in the late 1920s, they were still based in sandlots rather than any professional league. Many of Pittsburgh's finest young players were on the team, but the professional team across the river, the Homestead Grays, remained a cut above.

The Crawfords, or Craws as they were sometimes called, did attract large crowds. Most of their games were played at Ammon Field on the North Side. Instead of purchasing tickets for admission, game organizers passed a hat around to collect small donations from the fans. The money they collected was used to pay the players. On a good day, there might be a few extra dollars in their pockets.

The Crawfords played as many as a hundred games in a summer. They established a reputation in the African American baseball world, even getting a mention every now and then in Pittsburgh's African American newspaper, the *Pittsburgh Courier.* Nevertheless, they made little money.

The Great Depression that began in 1929 had a severe impact on organized African American baseball. A team like the Craws suffered greatly, as fans had little money to

The Man, the Myth

Perhaps the greatest part of Gibson's legend is the many myths and stories regarding the length of his home runs. One tall tale has it that he hit a ball out of sight one day, only to have it reappear the next day. The umpire supposedly remarked, "Yer out! Yesterday, in Pittsburgh!" There are more believable stories of games being stopped midway to enable officials to measure one of Gibson's homers. The mayor of Monessen, Pennsylvania, did so one day, measuring one at a distance of 512 feet, a homer Gibson would later recall as the farthest he had ever hit. From New York's Yankee Stadium to Cincinnati's Crosley Field to Cleveland's Municipal Stadium, Gibson hit home runs farther than anyone.

donate. People still enjoyed watching games, but an African American team could no longer expect more than a penny or two, if that, from spectators.

But in 1930,. Gibson was still playing ball, smashing home runs all over Pittsburgh as the full-time catcher for the Colored Giants. He hit home runs farther than anyone else playing at the nonprofessional level. Legend of his power spread throughout the state of Pennsylvania. His home runs were sometimes written about in the *Courier,* bringing Gibson to the attention of many people, including the ones behind the famed Homestead Grays. At the time, though, there just wasn't space for him on the Grays' squad: as Judy Johnson, manager of the Grays in 1930, said of Gibson: "I had never seen him play but we had heard so much about him. Every time you'd look in the paper, you'd see where he hit a ball 400 feet, 500 feet. So the fans started wondering why the Homestead Grays didn't pick him up. But we had two catchers. Buck Ewing was the regular catcher, and Vic Harris, an outfielder, used to catch if we were playing a doubleheader."

Gibson did eventually make the Crawfords and can be seen here second from the left with center fielder Oscar Charleston, first baseman Ted Page, and third baseman Judy Johnson at a game in 1940.

The Making of a Home-Run Hitter

Much of what made Gibson a great ballplayer, and what separated him from most of his teenage friends playing in the sandlot leagues, was his intense study of the game. Gibson buzzed like a fly around as many games as he could watch. He studied the technical aspects of the game: pitching angles, batters' stances, throwing movements, and so on. Less interested in watching towering home runs soar out of the ballpark, Gibson liked to watch the players to see how they positioned themselves. He noticed how they changed position as each new batter approached the plate. Baseball was, Gibson realized, a game of strategy.

Gibson observed catchers in particular. He watched how they shifted their feet and talked to the infielders, giving them instructions; he heard the banter that catchers engaged in with batters in order to get inside their heads. His fascination with the game also extended to hitting. While he studied batters, his talents at the plate gave him confidence that he was close to having all of the tools he needed to be a great hitter.

Gibson's hitting style, in contrast to many African American players of his era, was nearly perfect. Many great African American players had never had the opportunity to learn the fundamentals of hitting form from a hitting coach, instead picking up their style from watching sandlot games and adopting the bad habits of other players. Gibson learned to hit in the same way he learned to catch: he studied, studied, studied.

Gibson patterned his style after that of the Yankees' first baseman, Lou Gehrig, whom Gibson felt was the most polished hitter of his day. Perhaps Gibson's only defect was his batting stance—an upright, flat-footed posture that he didn't really budge from when he swung the bat. But even this flaw was corrected not long into his professional career. His technical skill, combined with his unparalleled power and speed, made him a menace.

Gibson was not only a great home-run hitter, but a good overall hitter as well. He reached base often. Gibson had great courage at the plate, never letting a ball pitched at his head or an opposing catcher's remarks keep him from his task. Unlike many of today's baseball players, who celebrate as they round the bases after hitting a home run, Gibson played the game with a natural modesty. While his withdrawn nature dignified him among his peers, it would later hamper his contract negotiations.

Chapter 3

Playing with the Homestead Grays

Gibson proved himself to be a phenomenal hitter, but like any player, he struck out occasionally. His talents frustrated most opponents, but some similarly talented pitchers learned Gibson's batting style and were able to strike him out more often than not. Teddy "Big Florida" Trent of the American Giants and Chet Brewer of the Chicago American Giants and the Kansas City Monarchs were two such pitchers. Both could sometimes get the best of Gibson, though Brewer did say that he never really believed he had any significant success against the power hitter. According to Brewer, "[Gibson] could hit any pitch to any field. The only way to pitch to him was to throw the ball low and behind him."

There was one pitcher who got the best of Gibson on a regular basis: Satchel Paige. Arguably the only Negro League player more famous than

Gibson himself. Paige was a legendary pitcher who played over twenty seasons in the Negro Leagues. Many consider him to have been one of the best pitchers of all time for his long career and the huge crowds of fans he brought to the field. Gibson said that his hits off Paige were "few and far between." A duel ensued when the two, who would later become teammates for a few seasons, faced off. Their famed showdowns fill African American baseball history and created some of the most dramatic moments in the game. Gibson had a lot of respect for Paige's talent as a pitcher, but Paige also recognized Gibson's ability to turn things around in a hurry. "You look for his weakness, and while you're lookin' for it, he liable to hit forty-five home runs," Paige once said.

Gibson Joins the Grays

The myth and legend of Josh Gibson and his baseball talent began on the sandlots of Pleasant Valley. But the story, or stories, of how he became a member of his favorite team, the Homestead Grays, is the most complicated and enduring tale of all. According to legend, it was a series of freak accidents at a Grays night game that led Josh Gibson to the team.

Grays manager Judy Johnson tells one version of the story. Gibson started with the team in Pittsburgh on July 25, 1930, during a game between the Grays and 1929 Negro National League champions the Kansas City Monarchs. It was a night game under the unsteady lights of the Monarchs' new portable lighting system.

Johnson notes: "Joe Williams was pitching that night and we didn't know anything about lights. We'd never

Satchel Paige of the Kansas City Monarchs and Josh Gibson talk before a game in 1941. Paige and Gibson were teammates for a few seasons, but more often than not they played against each other.

played under 'em before, and we couldn't use the regular catcher's signals because if he put his hand down, you couldn't see it. So we used the glove straight up for a fastball and the glove down—that was supposed to be the curve. Some was Joe Williams and the catcher [getting] crossed up. The catcher was expecting the curve, and Joe threw the fastball and caught him right there, and split the finger. Well, my other catcher was Vic Harris, and he was playing the outfield and wouldn't catch. So Josh was sitting in the grandstand, and I asked the Grays' owner, Cum Posey, to get him to finish the game. So Cum asked Josh would he catch, and Josh said, ' Yeah, oh yeah!' We had to hold the game up until he went into the clubhouse and got a uniform. And that's what started him out with the Homestead Grays."

As the story goes, Gibson didn't get a hit that night, but he made no errors behind the plate. This was quite a feat, given that Gibson was still a raw, unformed player, and eighteen years old to boot. Gibson stayed on with the team, progressing very quickly as a catcher and hitter.

A more likely version of how Gibson ended up playing for the Grays claims that Cum Posey knew of Gibson and

Satchel Paige

Satchel Paige is often considered one of the best pitchers in the history of baseball. Born in 1906 in Alabama, he played in the Negro Leagues for twenty-two seasons before becoming the oldest rookie in Major League Baseball history after joining the Cleveland Indians in 1948 at the age of 42. He had a big personality and was known to pull crowd-pleasing stunts on the field that humiliated his opponents and highlighted his immense talents. Paige developed a number of different pitches over his career, many of which he invented after an arm injury in 1939 forced him to change up his pitching style. By the end of his career, he could throw nearly any possible pitch. Paige retired from playing in 1966, and in 1971 he became the first person elected to the Baseball Hall of Fame by the Committee on Negro Baseball Leagues. Paige passed away in 1982 at the age of seventy-five.

told him to be prepared to play in a Grays game at any time. Gibson made his debut during a twilight doubleheader against Dormont, a white semiprofessional team. Some of the particulars mirror Johnson's account: Buck Ewing did split a finger, and Posey did turn to his backup, Vic Harris, to catch until Gibson could be reached and arrive at the field. Posey had Harris's brother taxi over to Ammon Field, where Gibson was in the middle of a game playing for the Crawford Colored Giants. Gibson immediately withdrew from that game. After Gibson arrived, Posey put him into the Grays game with little fanfare. Whichever story is true, Gibson did join his beloved Grays that year. He split catching duties with Ewing and learned the art of "receiving," as catching is sometimes called, on the job.

A Strongman at the Plate

The stint with the Grays began Gibson's professional baseball career. Gibson spent a great deal of time traveling with the team across the country, and his teammates became more familiar to him than the fading image of his father, mother, siblings, and old friends on the North Side of Pittsburgh. This separation, especially from his family, became a major theme in Gibson's life. Barnstorming was the only choice Gibson and all African American players had if they wanted to make a living playing the game.

Though Gibson eventually developed into one of the greatest hitters in the history of baseball, he was still in need of development when he joined the Grays. But thanks to his single-mindedness about all things baseball, and his terrific—if raw—skills, he quickly became a star. W. Rollo Wilson, a writer for the *Philadelphia Independent*,

The Homestead Grays were originally based in the Pittsburgh area, but they eventually moved to Washington, DC, where this 1943 photo was likely taken.

summarized neatly what many were saying about Gibson at this early stage in his professional career: "Well, the kid could catch and did catch and is still catching. He's green yet, but the ripening process is moving apace. He has not mastered the technique in throwing to second base, but he kills off all the fast boys who try to steal. His stance at the plate is worse than Pimp Young's [another Grays catcher],

but he gets his base hits. His motto is—'a homer a day will boost my pay.'"

The papers labeled him "Samson," after the famed biblical strongman. Gibson's huge appetite for food, especially vanilla ice cream and hot dogs, was well known. Although he gained more and more attention, he always remained focused on the game. During his first season with the Grays, Gibson hit a home run in Yankee Stadium in the season-ending series against a good team, the New York Lincoln Giants. The home run reportedly traveled 500 feet into the bullpen in left field—a drive fans would claim for years was one of the longest home runs ever hit there, even longer than any by Babe Ruth or Mickey Mantle. Some people contend that the shot traveled out of the stadium, a feat no one had ever accomplished.

Though we will probably never be certain whether Gibson hit a ball out of Yankee Stadium, Jack Marshall, of the Chicago American Giants, claims he saw him do it: "In 1934, Josh Gibson hit a ball off of Slim Jones in Yankee Stadium in a four-team doubleheader that we had there... They say a ball has never been hit out of Yankee Stadium. Well, that is a lie! Josh hit the ball over that triple deck next to the bullpen in left field. Over and out! I will never forget that because we were going down to Hightstown, New Jersey, to play a night game and we were standing in the aisle when that boy hit this ball!"

Tragedy Off the Field

It was in 1930 that Gibson endured serious personal problems. He had met Helen Mason, who was from the Hill District in Pittsburgh. A few months younger than Josh, Helen became pregnant just after her seventeenth birthday. She and Josh married. Though still working an assortment of odd jobs, Gibson was quickly making baseball his main focus. The two lived in relative comfort and peace with Helen's parents. That August, Helen went into a difficult labor at Pittsburgh's Magee Hospital, and after delivering twins, lapsed into a coma and died a few hours later.

The baby girl, Helen, and boy, Josh Jr., were a welcome addition after Helen's death, but the children were raised primarily by Helen's parents, as Gibson had little time to care for them. As Josh Jr. got older, he served as a bat boy for

Gibson was known as a slugger who often hit home runs, and he was one of the most powerful hitters in the Negro Leagues. Here, he stands in a batting stance wearing a Homestead Grays uniform.

At the 1944 East-West All-Stars Game at Comiskey Park in Chicago, Illinois, Josh Gibson slides into home base. Unfortunately, he was tagged out by catcher Ted Radcliffe (standing).

some Grays' home games. Though a source of conflict for Gibson over the course of his career, his inability to care for and see his children became a matter of fact. He was, for all intents and purposes, an absentee father until the day he died. Gibson's devotion in life was to baseball and little else, a fact that his family endured.

That fall, Gibson began what would become a yearly ritual of cross-country exhibition games against white major league "All-Star" teams. These teams were usually composed of a haphazard collection of forgettable white players teamed with a top-name star or two, such as pitcher Dizzy Dean or hitter Jimmie Foxx.

The games served to contrast the styles of African American and white baseball. The African American baseball player, as the historian Robert Peterson notes, "had retained the gambling, rough, unorthodox style of play reminiscent of the days when [Ty] Cobb flew into second basemen with his spikes high and razor sharp. African American pitchers threw more and different pitches, including those delivered with a ball greased, cut, coarsened, or in some way 'doctored.' They devised every motion conceivable: side winder deliveries, submarine, cross-fire, even countless versions of hesitation pitches. Rules were arbitrary or not at all enforced, the only object was to win by getting the batter out."

African American players also played with a reckless but skilled style that the white players hadn't seen in years in their own leagues. Called "tricky baseball," the rules of strategy and logic were considered an inconvenience and weren't always followed. Bunts, intentional walks, and pick-off plays came at odd moments. This was all a stark contrast to the much more subdued game of the white players.

Racism on the Field

Despite the segregation of African American and white players at this time, and the routine racism that African American players experienced from many white players and white fans, a certain respect developed between African American and white ballplayers. White stars such as Dean and Foxx often praised certain African American players or the African American style of play to the press. The great pitcher Walter Johnson had this to say about Gibson: "There is a catcher that any big league club would like to buy for $200,000. His name is Gibson...he can do everything. He hits the ball a mile. And he catches so easy, he might as well be in a rocking chair. Throws like a rifle. Bill Dickey isn't as good a catcher. Too bad this Gibson is a colored fellow."

Generally though, anti-African American sentiment among most major leaguers, especially among team owners, was overwhelming. Luckily, Gibson, like many

Disrespect and Discrimination

One of the most notable examples of a racist white player who hated African American players was Chicago White Stockings (later the White Sox) star Cap Anson. Anson played in the 1880s and 1890s, and was the first player to reach 3,000 career hits. Anson led a campaign against the presence of African American players in the major leagues at the time. In 1887, before his White Stockings were to play the New York Giants, who were led by African American pitching power George Stovey, Anson announced that his team would refuse to play against a team that fielded an African American player. The game didn't take place, and Anson's continued efforts over the years helped to keep African American players out of the major leagues for a long time.

Adrian "Cap" Anson was a Major League Baseball player in the early twentieth century. Many people believe that Anson's racist attitudes played a major role in establishing the racial segregation of the MLB.

African American players, found some respite from this racism south of the border. Black players often played professional ball in Latin America in order to make enough money to live on, as they were paid significantly less than their white peers. But one upside of playing in places like Mexico and Cuba was these countries often had much less obvious racism than the United States. Upon completing his first season with the Grays, in 1930, Gibson began what would become another yearly ritual: He played winter ball in South America. When the season in South America ended, he returned to Pittsburgh to work odd jobs. But in the baseball world, he was well on his way to being a household name.

Chapter 4

Making a Living in the Negro Leagues

The only white player who came close to matching Gibson's strength at bat was the legendary Babe Ruth. In fact, at the time many members of the press referred to Gibson as the "Black Babe Ruth," and numerous historians still refer to him this way. Some, including Gibson's son, Josh Jr., have pushed back against this nickname since it seems to minimize Gibson's own achievements when compared to Babe Ruth's. As Josh Gibson Jr. has said, "Why do they say Josh Gibson is the Black Babe Ruth? Why don't they say Babe Ruth is the white man's Josh Gibson?"

In any case, Gibson was known as one of the most powerful sluggers in the Negro Leagues. In the 1931 season, when he was still playing with the Grays, Gibson was credited with hitting seventy-five home runs, two more than the record-breaking Barry Bonds of the San Francisco

Giants hit in 2001. As with all Negro League records, that mark is hard to verify, as league regulations differed and recordkeeping was limited in Gibson's day. By the end of his second year with the Grays, however, Gibson was known as a superstar on the field.

Greenlee, the Craws, and the Grays

An important development in Gibson's career occurred in 1931, when the then unknown businessman and gambler William A. "Gus" Greenlee purchased the Crawford Giants—the same sandlot team Gibson had helped to create and played for three years earlier. Greenlee had flash and a great sense of showmanship that he brought to the game of baseball. Later in 1931, Greenlee purchased the contract of Satchel Paige from the dissolved Cleveland Cubs for $250. This sum represented a significant increase in the salaries the current Giants were making and was a sign of Greenlee's willingness to spend money in order to win.

Greenlee's next order of business further confirmed his bravado and commitment to African American baseball. At that time, African American baseball teams played their games in ballparks owned by white teams. The African American team would arrange, with a white owner, to play their games on the days when white teams were out of town. These teams paid a rental charge and often a percentage of the gate receipts to the white owner. Greenlee, who was already establishing himself not only as a team owner but also as an African American rights activist, took his team ownership to the next level: He built his team a stadium, Greenlee Field, with $100,000 out of his own pocket.

Babe Ruth is one of the most famous baseball players ever. A power hitter and outfielder, Ruth played MLB for twenty-one years, most of which were spent with the New York Yankees.

The "White Josh Gibson"

Babe Ruth, born George Herman Ruth in Baltimore, Maryland, in 1895, is one of the most famous players in Major League Baseball history. He began his professional baseball career with the Baltimore Orioles at just nineteen as a pitcher and moved up to the majors when he joined the Red Sox later that year. He soon started to gain fame for his pitching, but people were also impressed by his hitting ability, particularly his tendency to hit home runs. In late 1919, Ruth's contract was sold to the New York Yankees, and he would play with them for the the next fifteen seasons. His reputation as a slugger grew, and Ruth continued to hit home runs with impressive frequency. In 1936, he became one of the very first five players inducted into the Baseball Hall of Fame. Ruth continued to be a big presence in the baseball world until he was diagnosed with cancer in 1946, and he passed away two years later in his sleep.

The Pittsburgh Crawfords were one of the only Negro League teams to have their own stadium: Greenlee Field. Gus Greenlee bought the land for Greelee Field and had a 7,500-capacity stadium built in 1932.

In 1932, Greenlee hoped to acquire the cream of Negro League baseball players. He raided the Homestead Grays, signing Oscar Charleston to be the Craws' player-manager. He snared the Grays' third baseman Judy Johnson, outfielder Ted Page, and added pitcher Sam Streeter. He then set his sights on Josh Gibson.

Greenlee and Cum Posey, the owner of the Grays, were two of the biggest names in African American baseball. Knowing that Greenlee would approach Gibson with an irresistible deal, Posey offered Gibson a contract the night before Greenlee did. Gibson signed the contract, thus (Posey thought) ensuring Gibson's presence on the Grays' 1932 roster. But Gibson broke his contract with Posey after Greenlee approached him again. The lure of a little more money, a new ballpark, and the vitality that always accompanies the start of a new team proved too strong. Gibson boarded a bus and headed to Hot Springs, Arkansas, to begin spring training with the Crawfords.

The Craws were an independent team, meaning they did not have to play an organized schedule of games. Greenlee felt that more money could be made if the team's schedule remained flexible. The team traveled in a flashy new bus Greenlee had purchased, and employed a historian to keep records of all their games and send news dispatches back to Pittsburgh-area papers. The legend of the Crawfords spread rapidly, and the Craws played 94 games in 109 days between March 25 and July 21, 1932. They logged 17,000 miles on the road and headed north to Pittsburgh for a dramatic match against the Grays.

Pittsburgh-area fans, writers, and players eagerly anticipated the five-game series between the Craws and Grays. Greenlee and Posey undoubtedly saw the series as an opportunity for revenge. Despite losing players to Greenlee, Posey

Winters in Latin America

Players often played winter league games in Latin America in order to make ends meet, as their salary in the regular season was too low support them for the whole year. In 1933, Gibson, like many other African American players, spent the winter playing baseball in Latin America, joining white and Latino players from places like Mexico, Cuba, and Puerto Rico. It was a winter season of blind baseball in which players of all colors played on mixed teams. Many white players, while playing on the same field against their African American counterparts, came to realize that African American players were easily their equals. Gibson preferred Puerto Rico out of all the Latin American countries he played in during the off-season. He quickly became a hero to local fans, and eventually a monument to Josh Gibson was erected in center field of San Juan's Escambron Stadium, a place in which he had hit many tape-measured home runs.

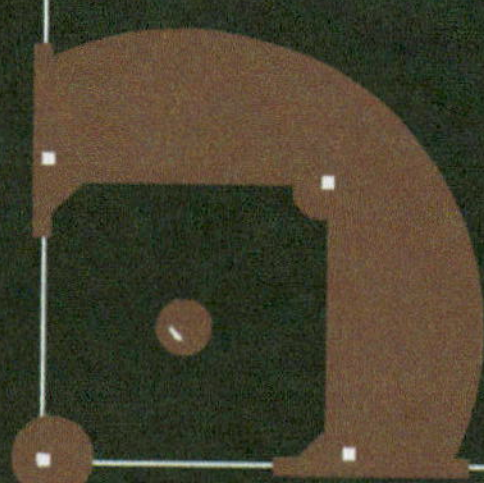

had put together a good team composed of wise veterans. In contrast, the Craws team was young and inexperienced, if exceptionally talented.

The series was evenly matched, and the Crawfords ended up winning three of five games. The 1932 series marked the beginning of a great rivalry that revved up local fans and infused African American baseball with a much-needed vitality. Posey couldn't deny that the advent of the Crawfords was beneficial for his team, especially since whenever the two teams played, he made the most money.

Tough Times in the Negro National League

In 1933, Greenlee decided to form a new league. He brought Posey's Grays team, along with several other established teams, into what he called the Negro National League. However, African American and white team owners alike were feeling the effects of the Depression. Babe Ruth, the highest-paid baseball player by far, took a $25,000 pay cut that year. Greenlee and other African American team owners realized that, despite the birth of their new league, the near future would be lean.

Times were tough, but they always had been, and for Gibson that just meant getting by and playing his beloved game. At the same time, Satchel Paige's fan and media appeal exploded. This brash, boisterous pitcher became the most famous African American player in the game. Sports writers loved him and his occasional crazy antics. He once left the Crawfords to take a bigger paycheck with a team in South Dakota, only to leave that team and rejoin the Craws. Although owner Greenlee was angry, he wouldn't dream of turning out his best pitcher and biggest draw.

This 1941 photo shows Gibson batting in the Puerto Rican winter league. Gibson's powerful home runs and excellent catching made him a popular player in the Negro Leagues for the sixteen years he played, from 1930 to 1946.

Gibson was much more subdued and was often called a "player's player" by his teammates, with whom he was very close. Though the press loved to write about Gibson's miraculous homers, he didn't draw crowds like Paige did. This would soon affect Gibson's professional fortunes.

With Paige and Gibson on the same team, something had to give. Gibson was a favorite of the other Craws, while Paige mostly kept to himself, a sign of his maverick personality. It became clear, at least to Greenlee, that one of them would have to be traded for financial reasons. Gibson was one of the top stars of African American baseball, perhaps the biggest next to Paige. Though he was the opposite in every way to the colorful Paige, Gibson was one of the league's greatest hitters and received nearly as much press coverage as Paige. In other words, Gibson knew his worth, or so he thought. One mistake Gibson made was in judging his worth as a player but not as an entertainer.

Nevertheless, Gibson's contribution to the Crawfords was immense. Because of the general lack of official records for nearly the entire history of Negro League seasons, relating Gibson's accomplishments on the field with certainty is difficult. Luckily, Greenlee had employed someone to keep track of the Crawfords' seasons. In 1933, Gibson played in 137 games for the Crawfords. He came to the plate 512 times. He had 239 hits, which gave him a batting average of .467, nearly 100 points higher than his next closest teammate. Gibson also led the team in triples and home runs (with 55), and he was second on the team in runs scored.

Waiting for a Worthwhile Offer

These impressive numbers reflect the importance of Gibson to a team that was already one of the best in Negro baseball—an importance not lost on Gibson. The average salary for an African American player during the Depression was a meager $125 a month, but Gibson was well paid, making $250 to $400 a month.

To some, however, the money that African American players made in comparison to their white counterparts was a product of something other than the economic hardship that had swept the country. Johnny Drew, the African American owner of the Philadelphia Hilldale team, put the blame on African American owners and players for underestimating their own worth. As he put it, "For [the African American ballplayer], there has never been any future, nobody has ever thought of making it possible for him to earn a salary of five thousand dollars a year. He has been exploited and bamboozled by the very men for whom he made fortunes in the past."

Drew also pointed to African American fans as part of the problem, calling them hypocrites for complaining about the increased price of admission to games—a move the owners had to make to attempt to break even. But these fans paid just as much money to attend games in which African American teams played white All-Star teams. In other words, the economics of African American baseball were complicated.

Regardless of the source of the economic problems African American baseball faced, the Crawfords were dangerously close to folding. The team had never turned a profit, despite their famous lineup and flashy showmanship.

CRAWFORDS of 193
3-18-32.

The Pittsburgh Crawfords at spring training in 1932. Gibson is third on the left in the the back row, the only one wearing a jacket over his uniform. His teammate and occasional rival, Satchel Paige, is standing second from the left, on Gibson's right.

By 1937, things worsened for the team, as a bidding war for Gibson's services began. While Gibson was in Puerto Rico playing winter ball, two teams, the Philadelphia Stars and the Homestead Grays, had offered Gibson different packages. The Stars offered Gibson a higher salary to be player-manager of their club. The Grays offered $2,500 and two players to the Craws in exchange for Gibson and Judy Johnson.

When Gibson returned home, he held out for the best offer, a fairly uncommon practice at the time and certainly out of character for him. Gibson realized that he had to take a stand. He wanted to obtain a contract that would pay him what he thought he was worth. He was tired of the long seasons, and he was being paid far less than what he was worth as the top hitter in the game. The hardball between Gibson and the Craws began.

In an attempt to lessen Gibson's value in the eyes of the public, and perhaps in Gibson's own eyes as well, John L. Clark, Greenlee's secretary and spokesperson, wrote the following in a column published in Pittsburgh's African American newspaper, the *Courier:* "He is an asset to any club. But not the kind of asset more colorful and less capable players might be. With all of his ability, he has not developed that which pulls the cash customers through the turnstiles...although he has been publicized as much as Satchel Paige." Most people ignored these comments and felt that Gibson had proven his value. Finally, the Grays' offer came through, and Gibson became, in what the *Courier* called "the biggest player deal in the history of Negro baseball," a Homestead Gray once again.

Chapter 5

Gibson's Tragic Decline

After five seasons with the Crawfords, Gibson was back with the Grays. His talents, combined with those of teammate Buck Leonard, helped the Grays win the league pennant for the next nine years. With the exception of a two-season stint playing in Mexico with the Azules de Veracruz, Gibson played on the Grays from 1937 to 1946, before his untimely death in 1947.

Despite the Grays' success over those nine years, Gibson's playing was not what it used to be. He had started to drink a lot more, and his personal life and health began to deteriorate significantly. Gibson was still a better hitter than most of his peers, but he wasn't anywhere near as good as he'd been as a young man. He'd been one of the greatest Negro League players ever—maybe even one of the best baseball players ever, period. But his last few years were marked by struggle and physical and emotional pain.

In Gibson's last years, his famous hitting became less reliable as his health began to deteriorate. This image was captured two years before Gibson's faceoff with Satchel Paige in the 1942 Negro League World Series.

Gibson Strikes Out

Many people mark a specific moment in 1942 as the beginning of Gibson's downward spiral, a moment some might call the most critical in all of African American baseball history. It was the Negro League World Series in 1942. The competing teams were the Kansas City Monarchs, led by Satchel Paige, and the Homestead Grays with Josh Gibson as their undeclared, quiet leader.

The Monarchs, thanks to Paige's superb pitching, easily won Game 1, 8-0. In Game 2, Paige came on to pitch,

Josh Gibson's Key Career Statistics

Seasons played: 1930-1946, Homestead Grays, Crawford Giants

Lifetime batting average: .347

Career home runs: 962

Number of All-Star appearances: 9

Number of pennants: at least 7

Career batting average in All-Star games: .483

Home run championships: 9

Batting titles: 4

relieving Hilton Smith. The Monarchs led 2-0. In the seventh inning, Paige gave up a single to Jerry Benjamin, and it was then that Paige's interior wheels began to spin. Always the showman, Paige called his first baseman, Buck O'Neill, over to the pitching mound and explained that he wanted to walk the next two batters, Howard Easterling and Buck Leonard. Paige wanted to face Josh Gibson with the bases loaded, creating in this one at-bat a defining moment in the history of African American baseball.

O'Neill couldn't believe what he was hearing, but the Monarchs' manager, Frank Duncan, who had also come to the mound, agreed with Paige. As he said, "Listen, Buck. You know all these people we got in this ballpark? They came out to see Satchel Paige and Josh Gibson. So whatever he wanna do, let him do it." Additionally, Paige knew something that most players, especially pitchers, had come to realize about Gibson. Unknown to most fans, Gibson was not the same hitter he had been several years before, when he seemingly had no fear at the plate.

Drinking and Drugs

Since Gibson had been playing winter ball in Latin America for most of his professional career, his trip to Mexico the previous winter, in 1941, was not unusual. Unfortunately, while he was there, his abuse of alcohol increased. While playing in Veracruz, he would sit in the dugout and drink one beer after another between games with his teammate, Sam Bankhead. Some also believe that Gibson had started to experiment with heroin at this time as well. By 1942, many noticed that Gibson had started to seem depressed.

Most evidence attributes this abrupt turn in Gibson's life to his failed relationship with a woman named Hattie, who lived with Gibson and had become his common-law wife. She had been effective, while they were together, in keeping Gibson together. When they separated, Gibson began an affair with a married woman from Washington, DC, named Grace Fournier. Fournier was a heavy drinker and known narcotics user, and it is suspected that Gibson had also picked up these habits.

Gibson often complained in those days of being tired and ill, and many people involved with the Grays commented that he looked nervous and bewildered most of the time. He had definitely changed, even his body. He went from being the lean, muscled athlete who used to inspire awe from all who saw him, to a heavy 225 pounds, with most of his weight seemingly contained in his belly. Cum Posey, who still owned the Grays, would let Gibson play even if he had been drinking, if only because he could still hit with the best of them. That year, Gibson had hit .323 in league games and led the league with 11 home runs in 41 games; the next year he led the league, reportedly hitting .521, with 14 homers.

But pitchers had learned of Gibson's self-destructive behaviors, and many players figured out that they could get into Gibson's head, make him think too much while at the plate, and strike him out. At least that is what Paige was thinking when he arranged to face Gibson with the bases loaded in the Negro League World Series.

Paige and Gibson Face Off

Legend has it that once Gibson got into the hitter's box, Paige began to distract him with trash talk. He would tell Gibson what kind of pitch he was going to make and where it would be placed. Gibson, unsure of Paige's words and just plain bewildered, watched three fastballs sail past him. He was out. According to the papers, Gibson had swung at two pitches, fouling off the first two, before swinging again and missing the third. Either way, one newspaper's headline the next day told the whole story: "Satch Fans Josh Gibson With Three on Bases."

This story is emblematic of the problems that Gibson faced throughout his life, particularly his baseball life. He was never quite able to get out from under Paige's shadow. Nor was he able to summon a suitable destiny for himself. Gibson's life was a series of painful episodes marked by an occasional high point on the ball field. His alcohol and drug problems and his physical deterioration made him vulnerable in such a competitive sport.

Gibson (*far right*) greets a few of his fans in 1942. Despite Gibson's personal and health problems, audiences still loved him.

A Deadly Diagnosis

New Year's Day, 1943. Gibson had been complaining of splitting headaches for a few weeks. He assumed the headaches resulted from his constant drinking binges. But on that day, he fell into a coma that lasted for six hours. His doctors at Pittsburgh's St. Francis Hospital publicly declared his problem to be exhaustion. Gibson left ten days later, and not much more was made of it.

Gibson took the advice of his doctors and manager and rested. He seemed to rebound that year, hitting .526 that season, and had a three-home-run game, including one that reportedly sailed 460 feet. Things seemed, if not great, then at least OK, except for his considerable drinking problem. He was still hitting balls all over the field, still playing in most of the Grays' games. To an outsider, Gibson probably seemed like the player he had always been.

But he was not. Though most of the people associated with African American baseball knew Gibson was having substance abuse problems—and most of them were upset that the player who represented all that was good in the league was in sharp decline—little about it was spoken outright. The next year, 1944, Gibson's power decreased dramatically. For the first time in his playing career, he became a "singles hitter." He was knocking fewer home runs, and many assumed that his power loss was due to drinking and aging.

Since Cum Posey tightly controlled press coverage about Gibson, the fans knew next to nothing about Gibson's decline. The papers reported that he was taking a "rest," when he was actually spending time in various sanatoriums closely monitored by doctors and nurses. Posey feared that

Gibson was losing his mind. These sanatorium visits soon became a regular part of Gibson's life.

As it turned out, exhaustion had not caused Gibson's New Year's Day blackout. Doctors informed him that he had a brain tumor. Gibson never let on about this fact, and he continued to play when he could. Unfortunately, he also continued to shoot heroin and drink, often getting into trouble with police, who frequently took him away in a straitjacket.

Gibson continued to miss more games, including the 1945 East-West All-Star Game. Apparently, he hadn't been able to find his way to Chicago, where the game was played. Gibson also became suicidal. He began talking to imaginary people, and he continued drinking.

The End of an Era

Gibson played his last games in the fall and winter of 1946 in the Puerto Rican League, but his most notable times that season took place off the field in local bars, where he would drink himself into a rage and often end up in the local jail. These bouts with booze led to his arrest one evening after he was found walking naked through the streets in a daze. The police asked him what he was doing, and Gibson replied that he was trying to get to the airport. He was placed in a local sanatorium, released, and sent back to Pittsburgh.

While Gibson spent the winter in Puerto Rico—and frequently in trouble—the American baseball world swelled with the anticipation that Jackie Robinson was going to join the Brooklyn Dodgers. Robinson was the first African American baseball player since Moses "Fleet" Walker to play in the major leagues. For a time, many felt that Gibson might be the first Negro League player to join the majors.

Gibson had wanted to play in the big leagues because it would have given him the chance to show the world that African American baseball players were the equals of, if not superior to, white players. Given a chance to cross the color line, it seems fair to say Gibson would have had an impact on the major leagues. But by the time white owners were beginning to seriously consider integrating their league, Gibson and other Negro League stars, like Satchel Paige and Cool Papa Bell, were nearing the end of their playing careers.

A Lonely Death

The end was near, and Gibson tried to reconnect with his family. He had barely seen his children during their childhood. Due in large part to Gibson's failure to offer any kind of financial support to his former mother-in-law, who was raising the children, they had grown up in poverty.

By 1947, Gibson was gravely ill, suffering from high blood pressure and bronchitis in addition to his other ailments. He had moved into his mother's house, back home in Pittsburgh's North Side. A few weeks later, on Sunday, January 19, Gibson went to see a movie at the Garden Theater and fell unconscious in his seat. He died in his bed at 1:30 AM the next day, with his sister, Annie Mahaffery, and his younger brother, Jerry, at his side. The cause of death, as filed by the doctor on the scene, was a stroke. Gibson died young, poor, and in many ways, alone. Though his family was with him, he barely knew them.

His funeral attracted numerous ball players, word of his death having spread quickly across the country. Though

Gibson rounds the bases in a 1943 game against the Baltimore Elite Giants. Even in his final years, Gibson was a formidable player.

some players were still in Latin America playing winter ball, many of Gibson's teammates attended his funeral. Many reporters claimed that Gibson had died of a broken heartand that he was bitter because he had never been able to play alongside his white peers. If Gibson died of a broken heart, it is likely that his sadness was due more to his distant relationship with his family, especially his children. In either case, the world of baseball, African American and white, had lost one of its greatest players.

The Hall of Fame

On August 9, 1971, Satchel Paige became the first Negro Leagues player elected into Major League Baseball's Hall of Fame. Six years earlier, the splendid white player Ted Williams was inducted to the Hall of Fame. During his induction speech, Williams remarked, "Baseball gives every American boy a chance to excel. This is the nature of man and the name of the game. I hope that some day Satchel Paige and Josh Gibson will be voted into the Hall of Fame as symbols of the great Negro players who are not here only because they weren't given the chance."

Jackie Robinson had crossed the color line years before and had been inducted into the Hall of Fame in 1962. Many Latino and African American players had long and impressive major league careers after him, among them Hall-of-Famers Frank Robinson, Willie Mays, Hank Aaron, and Roberto Clemente. But finally, in 1969, the Baseball Writers Association, the group that voted members into the Hall, created a special Negro Leagues panel in order to redress these grievances. Satchel Paige, African American baseball's most famous son, was the logical first choice.

Since Paige's election, sixteen more Negro League players have been elected into the Hall of Fame, including Josh Gibson, who was elected the following year. The Baseball Hall of Fame Committee on Baseball Veterans, a panel comprised of writers and Hall of Fame players that votes on players overlooked in the regular polling, took over the duties of the Negro Leagues panel. In a special amendment to the Veterans Committee rules, two special elections were held each year from 1995 through 1999, one of which was exclusively for Negro League players. That term was extended two years and still existed as of the 2001 elections, when Smokey Joe Williams was elected.

The Gibson family—Josh Jr. and his family, and Josh Sr.'s sister, Annie—accepted the posthumous tribute to Gibson in 1972 at the Hall of Fame in Cooperstown, New York. They called Gibson's induction "a beautiful thing" and made their way back to Pittsburgh, where life was still tough and they still lived in poverty.

Black Players in Today's MLB

Today, baseball seems to have overcome many of racism's effects. White players are now in the minority in professional baseball. In addition to the talented African American and Latino players, many Asian players, such as Hideo Nomo and Ichiro Suzuki from countries like Korea and Japan, where baseball is a huge national pastime, have made their way onto major league rosters. Jim Crow grudgingly disappeared off state law books; civil rights became a national issue. The playing field, perhaps, has been leveled. But this is not to say that racism does not exist in American baseball, or in America in general.

Some of the most famous players of the last ten years, including David Ortiz, Alex Rodriguez, and Derek Jeter, could not have played in the major leagues sixty years ago because of racism. Today, they are embraced by fans and have made millions playing the sport. But the percentage of Major League Baseball players who identify as African

GRAYS

The president of the Josh Gibson Foundation, Gibson's great-grandson Sean, points out artifacts in the 2007 exhibit on Josh Gibson at the Mayflower Hotel in Washington, DC.

The Negro Leagues Baseball Museum

The Negro Leagues Baseball Museum (NLBM) opened in Kansas City, Missouri, in January 1991. Located in the historic Vine District adjacent to the Jazz Museum, the NLBM has become an important voice in the preservation of African American baseball history. Though it is not an official hall of fame, the museum features a 10,000-square-foot multimedia exhibit that includes two film exhibits, two video exhibits, and fifteen interactive computer stations. The museum's gallery is arranged as a timeline of African American and baseball history from the 1860s to the 1950s. The centerpiece is the "Field of Legends," which features twelve life-sized bronze cast sculptures of the most important players in the history of the Negro Leagues. The statues stand at each position on the field, and the one behind the plate depicts the greatest catcher in African American baseball, Josh Gibson.

American is still low. In the 1980s, nearly 20 percent of MLB players were African American. In the past few years, that number has dipped below 10 percent. Teams are trying to remedy this by recruiting more young black players, but the issue of accessibility remains.

Josh Gibson's Legacy

Next time you're watching your favorite baseball team, whether on television or at the ballpark, think about Josh Gibson, the Negro Leagues, and how far today's players of color have come in the struggle for integration. The importance of Gibson's determination, integrity, and awesome skill can't be underestimated. The legacy of Josh Gibson remains with us in many ways: in the historical marker the city of Pittsburgh created in his honor, for instance, and in the Josh Gibson Little League.

Perhaps most important, the memory of Josh Gibson is preserved in Pittsburgh with each swing that every black player takes, whether in the big leagues or to knock a pitch across a dusty sandlot as the sun sets and dinnertime approaches. Josh Gibson and the Negro Leagues will forever hold a place in the history of baseball.

Negro Leaguers in the Hall of Fame

NAME	POSITION	PRIMARY TEAM	DATE INDUCTED
Satchel Paige	Pitcher	Kansas City Monarchs	1971
Josh Gibson	Catcher	Homestead Grays	1972
Buck Leonard	First Baseman	Homestead Grays	1972
Monte Irvin	Left Fielder	Newark Eagles	1973
Cool Papa Bell	Center Fielder	St. Louis Stars	1974
Judy Johnson	Third Baseman	Hilldale Daisies	1975
Oscar Charleston	Center Fielder	Pittsburgh Crawfords	1976
Martín Dihigo	Pitcher	Cuban Stars	1977
Pop Lloyd	Shortstop	New York Lincoln Giants	1977
Rube Foster	Pitcher/Manager	Chicago American Giants	1981
Ray Dandridge	Third Baseman	Newark Eagles	1987
Leon Day	Pitcher	Newark Eagles	1995
Bill Foster	Pitcher	Chicago American Giants	1996
Willie Wells	Shortstop	St. Louis Stars	1997

NAME	POSITION	PRIMARY TEAM	DATE INDUCTED
Bullet Rogan	Pitcher	Kansas City Monarchs	1998
Joe Williams	Pitcher	New York Lincoln Giants	1999
Turkey Stearnes	Center Fielder	Detroit Stars	2000
Hilton Smith	Pitcher	Kansas City Monarchs	2001
Frank Grant	2nd Baseman	Cuban Giants	2006
Pete Hill	Center Fielder	Chicago American Giants	2006
José Méndez	Pitcher	Cuban Stars	2006
Louis Santop	Catcher	Hilldale Daisies	2006
Ben Taylor	First Baseman	Indianapolis ABCs	2006
Sol White	Second Baseman/ Executive	Philadelphia Giants	2006
Ray Brown	Pitcher	Homestead Grays	2006
Willard Brown	Outfielder	Kansas City Monarchs	2006
Andy Cooper	Pitcher	Kansas City Monarchs	2006
Biz Mackey	Catcher	Hilldale Giants	2006
Mule Suttles	First Baseman	Newark Eagles	2006
Cristóbal Torriente	Center Fielder	Chicago American Giants	2006
Jud Wilson	Third Baseman	Philadelphia Stars	2006

Timeline

1846

The first recorded baseball game takes place between the Knickerbocker Base Ball Club of New York and the New York Base Ball Club, at Elysian Fields in Hoboken, New Jersey.

1911

December 21: Josh Gibson is born in Buena Vista, Georgia.

1920

Under the guidance of Rube Foster, team owners organize the first successful African American professional league, the eight-team Negro National League.

1923

Gibson and his family move to Pittsburgh, Pennsylvania.

The Eastern Colored League is formed.

1927

Gibson drops out of school after finishing ninth grade and begins his career with the Pittsburgh Crawfords.

1928

Gibson helps Harry Beale organize the Crawford Colored Giants.

1929

March 7: Gibson marries Helen Mason.

1930

July 25: Gibson plays his first game with the Homestead Grays.

August 11: Gibson's wife passes away while giving birth to Gibson's twin son and daughter, Josh Jr. and Helen.

1931

Gibson is credited with hitting seventy-five home runs while playing with the Grays in the 1931 season.

Gus Greenlee purchases the Crawford Giants.

1932

The Negro National League shuts down after twelve seasons.

Gus Greenlee's Craws and Cum Posey's Grays face off and begin a great rivalry.

1933

Gus Greenlee organizes the second Negro National League. The first Negro League All-Star Game takes place in Chicago.

Gibson meets Hattie Jones, his second (likely common-law) wife.

1934

Gibson allegedly hits a home run out of Yankee Stadium, a before unheard of feat.

1937

The Negro American League is formed with teams in Chicago, Kansas City, Detroit, Indianapolis, Cincinnati,

St. Louis, Memphis, and Birmingham. The Kansas City Monarchs win five of the first six NAL pennants. In the NNL, the Homestead Grays win eight pennants between 1937–1945.

1937

Gibson plays in the Dominican Republic for dictator Rafael Trujillo.

Gibson rejoins the Grays and helps bring them to the first of nine consecutive league pennants.

1938

Gibson wins his first batting title, with a batting average of .440.

1942

The Negro League World Series is played for the first time since 1927. The Monarchs sweep the Grays in four games.

1943

Gibson blacks out and is hospitalized on New Year's Day.

1944

Gibson meets Grace Fournier and begins an affair with her.

1945

Jackie Robinson signs a contract to play for the Brooklyn Dodgers' minor league team, the Montreal Royals.

1947

On January 20, Josh Gibson dies of a brain tumor only a month after his thirty-fifth birthday.

Jackie Robinson plays in the major leagues and wins the National League Rookie of the Year Award.

1949

The Negro American League absorbs the Negro National League, which folded in 1948 due to poor attendance and fewer quality players to choose from, as more and more African American players were jumping to the major leagues.

Josh Gibson Jr. starts playing with the Homestead Grays.

1963

The Negro American League folds. Organized African American baseball is relegated to a few traveling teams.

1972

Gibson is inducted into the Baseball Hall of Fame.

Glossary

amateur Done without the expectation of payment.

barnstorming Traveling to play exhibition games against local teams.

batting average A measure of a batter's performance taken by dividing the total number of hits by the number of times at bat, not including walks.

cricket A sport developed in England and popular across the world that is played with a bat and ball.

doubleheader When two games are played one after the other in the same place between the same teams.

gentleman's agreement An agreement that is not legally binding, often unspoken.

Great Depression The economic slump in North America, Europe, and other industrialized areas of the world that began in 1929 and lasted until about 1939. It was the longest and most severe depression ever experienced by the industrialized Western world.

induction The process of bringing someone into a group.

Jim Crow Any of the laws that enforced racial segregation in the US South between the end of the formal Reconstruction period in 1877 and the beginning of a strong civil rights movement in the 1950s.

marginalize To treat an individual or group as though they don't matter.

narcotic An addictive drug that in moderate doses dulls the senses, relieves pain, and induces profound sleep, but in excessive doses can cause stupor, coma, or convulsions.

pennant Winning the league pennant means that team is the league champion for that year.

prejudice Hatred or fear of an individual or group not based on reason or experience.

Reconstruction In US history, the period during and after the American Civil War (1865-1877) in which attempts were made to solve the political, social, and economic problems arising from the readmission to the Union of the eleven Confederate states that had seceded at or before the outbreak of war.

repeal To make invalid.

sanatorium An institution for rest and recuperation, often for the treatment of people with chronic illnesses, especially mental illnesses.

segregation Separation of groups of people from one another, especially based on race.

straitjacket A heavy jacket with straps to restrict the movement of arms, used to restrain violent or mentally ill people so that they can't hurt themselves or others.

suppression Forced ending of something. Voter suppression is the creation of laws or use of strategy to prevent certain people from voting.

Further Reading

Books

Democker, Michael. *Barnstorming.* Kennett Square, PA: Purple Toad Publishing, 2016.

Diprimio, Pete. *Legends of the Leagues.* Kennett Square, PA: Purple Toad Publishing, 2016.

Lester, Larry. *Black Baseball in New York City: An Illustrated History, 1885-1959*. Jefferson, NC: McFarland, 2017.

Panchyk, Richard. *Baseball History for Kids*. Chicago, IL: Chicago Review Press, 2016.

Sturm, James, and Rich Tommaso. *Satchel Paige: Striking Out Jim Crow*. New York, NY: Disney-Hyperion, 2019.

Websites

Josh Gibson Foundation

www.joshgibson.org

The Josh Gibson Foundation, founded by Josh Gibson Jr. in honor of his father, supports programs to help youths reach academic and athletic success.

Major League Baseball's "Negro Leagues Legacy"

mlb.mlb.com/mlb/history/mlb_negro_leagues.jsp

The official website of Major League Baseball offers a huge archive of Negro Leagues history and images.

National Baseball Hall of Fame

baseballhall.org/hall-of-famers

The Baseball Hall of Fame's official website has lots of historical articles and information about individual Hall of Famers to explore.

Negro Leagues Baseball Museum

www.nlbm.com/s/index.cfm

The Negro Leagues Baseball Museum was founded in 1990 and is located in Kansas City, Missouri.

Index